DISNEY
PRINCESS
BEGINNINGS

BELLE'S Discovery

BY TESSA ROEHL

ILLUSTRATED BY
THE DISNEY STORYBOOK ART TEAM

Random House 🏠 New York

'

For Mom and Dad

—T. R.

randomhousekids.com

Library of Congress Cataloging-in-Publication Data is available upon request.

ISBN 978-0-7364-3579-6 (trade) — ISBN 978-0-7364-8177-9 (lib. bdg.)

Printed in the United States of America

10 9 8 7 6 5 4 3 2 1

Book design by Jenna Huerta & Betty Avila

This book has been officially leveled by using the F&P Text Level Gradient™
Leveling System.

Random House Children's Books supportsthe First Amendment and celebrates
the right to read.

Chapter 1
The Inventor's Daughter

Belle shifted her doll so it faced the front of the classroom. Sharing her desk chair wasn't the most comfortable thing, but she'd do what Sylvie and the triplets did: sit hip to hip with their dolls in their cramped desks.

The special dolls were from Paris. Belle's friend Sylvie had been talking about hers for weeks. The other girls always seemed to be having such a good time, brushing the dolls' hair, making up stories about their lives, and trading the outfits they'd collected. Finally, Belle had a doll, too, and she was eager to join in the fun.

The night before, Belle had stayed up past her bedtime, making a few changes to her doll with her father's tools. She couldn't help it. Inspiration had struck. Her father always told her that when inspiration strikes, you must grab it.

"Monsieur Jacques!" Thomas called. "Belle took another trip to the clouds." He snickered, and Claudette, one of the triplets, joined him. Thomas was always poking fun at someone.

Belle startled. This wasn't the first time she had been caught in a daydream. But the teacher, Monsieur Jacques, never seemed to get angry with her. He winked and held up a piece of blank paper and a quill. It was time for math lessons, Belle's favorite part of class, after reading.

Belle reached for her schoolbag, nearly knocking her doll to the ground. She set the doll on her desk and took out a quill pen and paper. When she sat up, she noticed that the classroom had fallen unusually quiet. Thomas's cheeks were red from holding in another laugh. Claudette's nose crinkled, and Sylvie's hand was clasped over her mouth.

Everyone was staring at Belle's doll. Belle stared, too. There were the ears she'd cut into points. The purple skin she'd colored with her father's paint. And best of all, the wings she'd made from his leftover wire scraps. The doll was a fairy!

Belle nestled her fairy doll back beside her. *They're just surprised,* she thought. *They'll want to hear all about my doll after school.*

When class was over, the students gathered in the schoolyard as they always did to talk and play in small groups. Belle scanned the crowd for Sylvie and the triplets. It was never hard to spot the three sisters, with their identical outfits (though Claudette's was red, Laurette's orange, and Paulette's green) and sunny blond hair that hung past their waists. Sylvie's bright red curls always stood out, too—they practically matched Claudette's dress.

Sure enough, Belle saw the girls right away, whispering under a large tree. "Sylvie!" Belle called, and skipped toward her. Claudette nudged her sisters as Belle drew near. Then Claudette, Laurette, and Paulette walked away, leaving just an embarrassed Sylvie behind.

As the triplets crossed the schoolyard, Belle heard what they were saying. They certainly didn't try to keep their voices down.

"She's so peculiar. I can't imagine what goes through that head of hers!"

"She gets it from her father, you know. He's pretty batty, too."

"That's what happens when you don't have a mother."

The words pricked at Belle's heart. It wasn't the first time she'd heard other kids gossip about her, but she never got used to it. Especially when they talked about her father.

"The other girls don't like me very much, do they?" Belle said to Sylvie.

Sylvie shifted from one foot to the other. "I think they had to get home." But the triplets hadn't gone home at all. They had only moved to the bench across the schoolyard.

Sylvie took a deep breath. "It's just—Belle, why did you ruin that beautiful doll?"

Belle looked down at the doll in her arms. "Ruin?"

"You chopped up her ears and nose! You painted over her beautiful skin!" Sylvie cried.

Belle laughed. "No, she's not ruined." She placed the doll in Sylvie's hands. Sylvie looked at it as if Belle had handed her something rotten. "I'd just finished reading the most wonderful story about fairies, and then inspiration struck! She's so much more than a doll now. She's an invention!"

Belle pointed at the wings screwed into the doll's wooden back. "See? She can fly. I could help you and the triplets with your dolls. We could make them into princesses or witches or more fairies. There are so many options."

Sylvie held the doll up next to her own. "Belle . . . why do you try so hard to be different?"

"Different?" Belle didn't understand. "I'm not trying to be different."

Sylvie sighed. "If you want to get along

better with the other girls, it's really not so hard. When you start thinking about ways to be *inventive,* or how to do things *differently*" — she handed the doll back to Belle — "just stop and do the opposite." Sylvie walked over to join the triplets, her own "normal" doll in her arms.

Belle had started the day excited about her doll and the chance to spend time with the other girls. But now all her excitement had floated away like gossip whispered in the wind.

She began her walk home, shoulders slumped.

Chapter 2
Marked

Belle trudged up the steps to her cottage. She opened the door, and her father tumbled outside, much to her surprise.

"Papa!" Belle exclaimed as her father, Maurice, landed on his bottom at the foot of the stairs. She helped him up. "What were you doing at the door, anyway?"

"Working on my latest invention." Maurice led Belle inside. He yanked on a hunk of metal attached to the wall next to the doorframe. It moved with an accordion-like lever. "I call it the Invisible Eye. You can look through it and see who's at the door."

"But you didn't see me coming," Belle said.

Maurice's mustache twitched as he started to chuckle. "It's not finished, of course. But when it is, we'll be able to see all our visitors before they see us."

The invention didn't look like much. But Belle trusted her father and thought he was a genius. She grabbed her own invention from her bag. "Do you think my doll is ugly?"

Maurice frowned. "You worked so hard

on it last night. Why would you ask such a thing?"

"Sylvie and the other girls think I ruined it," Belle said.

"But you like the doll, don't you?" Maurice asked.

Belle nodded. "I do. I think it's beautiful."

Maurice ushered Belle toward the bench. "Let's sit for a moment," he said. Belle sat next to her father, and he curled his arms around her shoulders. The can of purple paint Belle had used to color her doll's skin was at their feet. "Have I ever told you how you got your name?" Maurice asked.

"No," Belle said.

"Your mother picked it."

"She did?" Belle smiled. She loved hearing stories about her mother.

"She did," Maurice said. "After you were born, when the doctor placed you in your mother's arms, she said she could think of only one word when she held you: *Belle*. She had never seen something as beautiful as you in all her life."

Belle closed her eyes. She tried to picture her mother gazing down at her and saying

"Belle." She wished she could remember the feeling of being in her mother's arms. But she had been too young when her mother died.

Suddenly, Belle felt something wet on her nose. She looked at her father, surprised to see a paintbrush in his hand. She tried to glance at the spot. "Papa! You painted my nose!"

"I certainly did," her father said.

"But why?" Belle tried to see the purple dot on her face.

Maurice grinned. "Because that mark makes you even more beautiful. Different and special from the inside out, just like your fantastic doll. And just like your mother, who you look and act more like every day."

Belle eyed her father suspiciously. "A purple mark does all that?"

"Yes. Because it's yours and only yours," Maurice said.

Belle smiled and hugged her father.

Chapter 3

A Revolution, a Race, and a Rescue

The next day at school flew by. Belle's conversation with her father had filled her with confidence and determination. She took her doll back to school and ignored the stares from Sylvie and the triplets. Belle was ready to find friends who would understand her and like her just the way she was.

When class was over, Belle looked

around the schoolyard to see who she could get to know better. She saw Nicolas and his older sister, Marian, talking excitedly. Belle loved how they always seemed excited about something. As she got closer, she heard them mention the country's capital.

"Did I hear you say Paris?" she asked. Belle loved to think about the world outside her village.

"Have you heard the word *revolution*?" Nicolas asked.

"Of course she hasn't, Nicolas," Marian said.

"Actually, I have. My papa told me about

it," Belle said. "It's when people are unhappy about something and want to change the way things are."

Marian looked impressed. "We're starting a revolution of our own. Will you join us?" she asked.

Belle was thrilled she had found people who wanted to talk about big ideas. "What are you revolting against?"

"Revolting! Ha! She called you revolting!" Marian laughed at Nicolas.

Nicolas ignored her. "We're starting with Gustave's Candy Shop!" he cried, raising a fist in the air.

"The candy shop?" Belle was confused. She didn't think the people in Paris were fighting about candy.

"That was *not* my idea, Nicolas," Marian said. "Our revolution isn't about candy—it's about the toy shop!"

Belle wasn't sure these were the big ideas she'd had in mind. She slipped away, leaving Nicolas and Marian to argue.

Belle spotted Thomas, Juliet, and some of her other classmates racing around the schoolyard. At least no one was fighting over there.

"What are you doing?" Belle asked Juliet.

"We're blind racing!" Juliet answered.

The racers were wearing blindfolds and running at top speed. As Belle watched them, she wished she had a blindfold, too, so she didn't have to see anyone get hurt. On the way to the finish line, one of the racers crashed into a tree, and another made a wrong turn and ran toward the school. Thomas was the only one who finished the race without injury.

"I'm in the next round." Juliet grinned at Belle. "Do you want to try?"

Belle noticed that Juliet's arms and legs were covered with scrapes and bruises. "Maybe next time," Belle said. Scraping up her knees was not her idea of fun.

Belle turned around to face the school-yard once again. She wanted to find someone she had at least one thing in common with. She spied Morton, who was sitting alone under a tree, plucking grass. He looked lost in thought. *Perfect!* Anyone who could get lost in thought had something in common with Belle. She hurried over and plopped down on the ground beside him. "*Bonjour,* Morton."

Morton glanced up from the grass. "*Bonjour* . . . Belle."

"I hope I'm not interrupting anything. I was just over with Nicolas and then Juliet and those racers, and . . . Everyone likes such different things, don't they?" Belle ran her hands through the grass. This did seem like a lovely thinking spot.

"I don't mean to be rude, but you are interrupting my thinking," Morton said.

Belle didn't know what to say. "I thought

we could talk about ideas or something. Or just think quietly."

"I do better thinking on my own. Don't you?" Morton asked. His eyes were kind enough, but he clearly did not want company.

"Perhaps I do. Enjoy your thinking." Belle stood up. Across the schoolyard she saw Sylvie and the triplets gathered on a bench, brushing their dolls' hair.

Belle sighed. Didn't she have anything in common with anyone?

On her way home, Belle passed the tavern, the bakery, and the butcher shop. She barely noticed the people strolling by, busy with their errands. Belle was busy, too. She was busy thinking about why she felt so alone.

The feeling had been bothering her for a while. It seemed like everyone Belle knew had something to do that didn't include her. Papa had his inventions. Sylvie and the triplets had their dolls. Nicolas and Marian had their arguments. Juliet and Thomas had their races. Belle didn't know where she fit in. She had her daydreams and her fairy doll, but they only led to teasing. There had to be someone to play with.

An awful animal shriek tore Belle away from her thoughts. She looked in the direction of the noise to see some classmates teasing a cat. Thomas was among them. They had surrounded the animal in an alley next to the abandoned bookshop. One of the girls was trying to tie a blindfold around the cat.

Belle ran over to them. "What are you doing?" she asked. The poor cat looked pitiful. He had several bald spots in his fur. One eye was clouded over. As he hissed, Belle saw that a few of his teeth were missing.

"Belle!" Thomas shouted. "This cat is so ugly, it reminds me of someone. Say, where is that doll of yours?"

Thomas's friends roared with laughter. The cat continued hissing.

"There's nothing wrong with being ugly,

Thomas. But there is something wrong with being cruel." Belle reached her hand out to the cat. He turned and ran toward the abandoned bookshop, disappearing through a basement window.

"I suppose you're going to rescue it now." Thomas chuckled. "Go on, then. It's only a haunted bookshop."

Belle stared at the bookshop entrance. A sign hung overhead. She could just make out the image of a book. Was the shop really haunted?

It didn't matter; the cat might need help. Belle could give him a home, and he could be her friend.

"I'm not afraid of ghosts,"

Belle said, sounding more confident than she felt. She approached the bookshop.

"Belle, I was only teasing. You don't have to go in there!" Thomas yelled. He sounded scared. But now that she was at the entrance, Belle felt as if going into the bookshop was something she needed to do.

She gripped the large handles and opened the doors.

Chapter 4
Abandoned?

The inside of the bookshop was like nothing Belle had imagined. She'd pictured a dark, empty place full of cobwebs, rats, and ghostly creatures. But she found none of those things. Instead there were more books than she had ever seen. More books than she even knew existed. Rows of shelves filled the center of the shop and lined the walls. It was as if she had stumbled upon a secret. Though the villagers may have abandoned the shop, the books hadn't gone anywhere.

Belle was itching to explore, but she had to find the cat first. "Here, kitty, kitty! I won't hurt you." She walked down an aisle, calling out for the cat. As she rounded the corner, she ran right into a person.

Belle jumped back and yelped. A woman stood in front of her, holding the cat.

"I'm not afraid of ghosts," Belle whispered to herself.

"*Ghost?* Do I look like a ghost?" The woman's silver hair was tied in a bun, and she was dressed in gray from head to toe. Even her eyes were gray.

Belle thought she did look a bit ghostly, but she didn't think it was possible for ghosts to hold cats. Also, the woman had felt solid when Belle had bumped into her. "No, Madame," Belle said. "But I didn't expect to find anyone here. I was following the cat. I thought the shop was abandoned."

"Well, you found me," the woman said. "And the cat."

Belle nodded toward the animal. "Is he yours? I thought he might be a stray."

"He belonged to my daughter. Now he belongs to the bookshop." The woman let the cat jump from her arms. He rubbed his cheek against Belle's ankle. Then he ran away, disappearing into the shelves.

"That's Tom for you. He always has somewhere better to be," the woman said.

"The cat's name is Tom?" Belle giggled

to herself. If Thomas only knew he shared a name with the cat!

"It wasn't my choice," the woman said, brushing the cat hair from her clothes. "It was kind of you to check on him. Have a good afternoon." She began to walk away.

"Wait!" Belle wasn't ready to leave. "Is this your bookshop?"

The woman turned. "It is. Hugo's Books. I'm Adèle Hugo, although no one calls me Adèle. I prefer Hugo."

"My name is Belle. Now that we aren't strangers, would you mind if I looked around? I know you're closed, but . . ." Belle hoped she wasn't asking for too much.

"The shop is not closed," Hugo said.

"It's not?" Belle was confused. *Why does everyone say it is?* she thought.

"What are your interests?" Hugo asked, changing the subject.

This was the very question Belle had been asking herself earlier today. She glanced at the doll in her arm. "Dolls, I guess." Belle wished she had a better answer.

Hugo took the doll from Belle's hands. Belle became worried. *What if Hugo thinks she's strange? What if she doesn't want me touching the books because of what I've done to my doll?*

Hugo handed the doll back to Belle.

"We have books about dolls. But that's no ordinary doll. It's a fairy."

Belle beamed. "It is. I made her that way."

Hugo studied Belle for a few moments. "Come with me," she said.

As Hugo led her through the aisles, Belle scanned the shop. Although it wasn't haunted or full of rats, the place did look like it had seen better days. Some of the lamps were broken. Shelves were crooked or missing. Several long, jagged cracks ran through the walls and ceiling. The stained-glass windows were dirty, and one was covered with boards.

Hugo stopped at a section of books against the right wall. "Someone who would

transform her doll to look like a fairy seems like someone who would enjoy fantasy and adventure books."

Belle had never been faced with so many choices. She used to just read and reread all her mother's old books. "Have you read any of these?" Belle asked Hugo.

"I've read every book in this shop," Hugo replied.

"Oh my!" Belle took a volume of fairy tales with a picture of a castle on the cover from the shelf.

Hugo watched Belle turn the pages. "Just a bit of advice, Belle. Enjoy the books. But don't let any of them muck up your head." With that, she walked away.

Muck up my head? Belle thought. What a funny thing to say. She sat down on the floor, leaned back against the shelf, and began to read. From the first sentence, she was in love.

"I was about to start supper without you," Belle's father said as she burst into the cottage later that evening. He was tinkering with his Invisible Eye invention.

Belle handed him a hammer. She always knew what tool he needed before he asked. "I made a discovery today," she said. "You know the abandoned bookshop? Turns out it's not abandoned!"

"Do you mean Roselle's Books?" Maurice asked, giving the Invisible Eye's lever a whack.

Belle made a face. "What? No, it's called Hugo's Books."

Her father peeked through the machine's eyehole. "One of the few things I heard about this village before we moved here was that it had a bookshop. The largest bookshop for miles." Maurice adjusted something on the contraption. "But when we arrived, all I found was a run-down building. The shop seemed to be a thing of the past. That was Roselle's Books. I'm not sure about this

Hugo fellow. They must've changed the name."

"It's a Hugo *lady,* Papa." Belle handed him another tool. "Can I go back tomorrow? And maybe the day after, too?"

Maurice smiled and nodded. "As long as you return by dinnertime."

Belle let out a squeal of excitement. "There are so many books there, and Hugo has read them all. She must know everything about the world. I wish I did, too," Belle said.

"Everything? That's a lot." Maurice laughed. "Here, take a look at our bit of the world." He lowered the Invisible Eye so Belle could peek through.

"I can see our front steps, Papa. It works!"
Belle loved it when her father finished an
invention. It made her feel as if anything was
possible.

"You have a lot to explore beyond this
cottage if you want to know everything
about the world. Explore until your heart is
full, Belle. And then explore some more." He
moved the Invisible Eye back into place. "You
should tell your friends about the bookshop.
They might like it, too."

Belle shook her head. "I don't think
they'll see it the way I do."

Maurice chuckled. "Don't give up on the
other children quite yet, my dear."

"Why not?" Belle asked.

"Do you give up on a book if you don't like the first chapter?"

Belle frowned. "I haven't found a book yet that I don't like."

Maurice began packing up his tools. "What about a book you don't understand?"

There were going to be plenty of those in the shop. But Belle had seen a dictionary when she was walking through. "I would get the dictionary to help me understand," she answered.

"That's my smart girl," Maurice said. "You always know how to find the tools to make things work."

Chapter 5
Roselle's Books

The next day in the bookshop, Belle went back to the book of fairy tales she'd started the day before. She read until it was dinnertime and Hugo closed up the shop.

Belle went back to the bookshop the next day and the next day and every day after that. She spent the first week in the fantasy and adventure section. The moment she finished one book, she picked up another. But soon she got curious about other subjects: history, romance, poetry, politics, comedy, tragedy. Some books were difficult to understand, but she tried anyway.

Every so often, Hugo would drop a book into Belle's lap. Those books always ended up being Belle's favorites. With each new story, Belle entered another world. She learned, laughed, cried, traveled, and lived a new life every day.

In school, Belle daydreamed even more than usual, waiting for class to end so she could return to the shop. Once, Sylvie asked her why she kept rushing off. "To read!" Belle answered.

"To read?" Sylvie asked, confused. Belle didn't have time to explain. She no longer cared whether Sylvie or her other classmates understood her. She had a new goal: to read every book in the shop, just like Hugo.

Hugo spent most of her time in the back room. No one else came into the shop except the delivery boy, who brought parcels of new books every so often. Belle didn't understand why Hugo didn't do something to let the village know the shop was still open. Or why she kept ordering books if there were no customers.

One day, Belle arrived at the bookshop with a jar of milk left over from her lunch. She thought Tom would enjoy it. She looked through the shop but didn't see the cat anywhere. When she reached the back, she noticed Hugo's door was cracked open. Belle knocked softly and pushed on the door to find a set of stairs leading down to the basement. "Hugo?" she called, but no one answered.

Belle made her way downstairs. Lining the walls were old clippings from the village newsletter. Each clipping mentioned a local bookshop event or special offer:

"Auction Saturday at Roselle's Books"

Roselle's Books, Belle thought. *That's the shop Papa mentioned.*

At the bottom of the stairs, Belle found a neat, cozy room with a desk, two chairs, and a small bookshelf. Hugo sat in one chair, reading, with Tom at her feet.

"Knock, knock," Belle said, holding up the bottle. "I brought Tom some milk."

Hugo pointed to a dish on the floor. "His saucer is there."

Tom opened his good eye to watch as Belle poured the milk. "Could I ask you a question, Hugo?"

Hugo glanced up from her book and nodded.

"What happened to Roselle's Books?" Belle asked.

"You're standing in it," Hugo said.

"But you said it was—"

"Hugo's Books. I know. Roselle was the old name. It was named after my daughter."

Belle didn't understand. "Why did you change it?"

Hugo frowned. "I'm not sure that's any of your business."

Belle felt her cheeks turn pink. "I'm sorry. I didn't mean to be impolite." She started back up the stairs.

"Belle," Hugo said. "I'm sorry."

Belle turned around. Hugo was gazing out the window. "I'm not used to anyone asking questions," she said. "It's been a long time."

"I hoped I could meet your daughter, but she's never come in," Belle said, stepping off the stairs and back into the basement.

Hugo shook her head. "She left years ago. Before you were even born."

"Where did she go?" Belle asked.

"She fell in love," Hugo said.

"Fell in love? That's wonderful." Belle didn't understand why Hugo sounded so sad. In the books Belle had been reading, love seemed like a form of magic.

"I named the bookshop after her because I believed she would take it over one day. I even planted a rosebush out back for her. She was the heart and soul of this shop. She organized events here and made friends with everyone in the village." Hugo laughed softly. "The shop was always full. It was a different time."

Belle nodded. These were the most words Hugo had ever spoken to her.

Hugo continued. "Those fairy tales you

like so much? They were Roselle's favorites, too. I'd always catch her sneaking down here to read." Hugo turned to the bookshelf. "But the stories weren't enough for her. One day a traveling salesman came through the village. He had journeyed all around the world, selling his wares. He promised my daughter adventures beyond the pages in books. In a matter of days they married, and she was gone."

"I'm sorry," Belle said. "You must miss her very much." She wanted to give Hugo a hug, but she wasn't sure Hugo was the hugging type. Instead she stayed still and listened.

"After Roselle left, I didn't come back to the shop for months. I didn't know how to run Roselle's Books without Roselle." Hugo's eyes became shiny. "When I finally returned, it seemed that the village had closed the shop for me. A window was broken. Paint was splattered over the outside. And, of course, the customers had stopped coming. It was Roselle they always came for anyway. She took her love with her, and it seems the shop needed it to survive."

"Do you know where she is?" Belle asked.

"She could be anywhere," Hugo said. "She sends letters twice a year. I stopped reading them."

Belle didn't know what to say to that. She couldn't imagine ignoring a loved one's letters.

A bell jingled upstairs. Someone had entered the shop.

Hugo frowned. "Stay here, Belle. I'll be right back." She went upstairs.

Who could that be? Belle wondered. Settling in to wait, Belle spotted a familiar book on a nearby shelf. It was the first book she'd read in the shop, the one with the castle on the cover. She picked it up, and a stack of papers fell onto the floor. As she kneeled to gather them, she saw that they were letters from Roselle. Hugo had kept the letters, even if she hadn't read them.

The sound of a strange woman's voice drifted down the stairs. Now Belle was very curious. If it wasn't the delivery boy, and it wasn't Hugo . . . *Could it be? Could Hugo's daughter have returned?*

She had to find out.

Chapter 6
Madame Beaumont

Belle crept up the stairs and tiptoed toward the voices at the front of the shop. She spied Hugo speaking to a woman Belle recognized from the village. The woman was wealthy, Belle knew that much. Her clothes were of the finest cloth and the latest fashion. Her face was pinched tight and covered with makeup. It wasn't Roselle.

"It's time, Hugo," the woman said.

"I don't know," Hugo replied.

The woman threw her gloved hands in the air. "You've been saying 'I don't know' for years now, as the cracks on the walls grow larger and your pocketbook grows smaller. No one comes into the shop anymore. The village has forgotten it."

Hugo lowered her head. "You're correct, Madame Beaumont. I can't deny that."

Madame Beaumont! Belle recognized that name. Beaumont Tavern. Beaumont Inn. The Beaumont family owned many of the buildings in the village.

"My offer won't last forever," Madame Beaumont said. "Sell me the building now, while it's still worth something."

Sell the bookshop? Belle bit her lip.

Hugo was quiet. "Let me have until the end of the month. Then I'll sign the papers," she finally said.

Madame Beaumont smirked. "You're doing the right thing. This village doesn't need a bookseller. But my social club does need an elegant place to meet."

Madame Beaumont started to leave, then turned and added, "Oh, and, Hugo. I expect every last book to be gone by the time I take over."

Belle rushed around the bookshelf to the next aisle. She no longer cared that she had been eavesdropping. She had to say something.

"Hugo! You can't sell the bookshop!"

Hugo calmly looked down at Belle. "I certainly can, Belle. It's my shop, and I can do what I want with it."

"But . . . the books. Where will the village buy its books?" Belle asked.

"The village doesn't buy its books here as it is," Hugo replied. "What's done is done."

"Please. I'll help you make the shop popular again. We can save it." Belle was pleading now, but she didn't know what else to do. She couldn't bear the thought of losing this place so soon after she'd discovered it.

Hugo's face went from calm to angry. "Belle, I tried to make this clear. Don't confuse the stories in these books with real life. The happy endings in fairy tales are fiction. The sooner you learn that, the better off you'll be." With those words, she turned on her heel and headed back to the basement.

Belle was crushed. She looked at the books around her. A thousand worlds right at her fingertips. Soon they would slip away, and Belle would be right back where she was before. Alone.

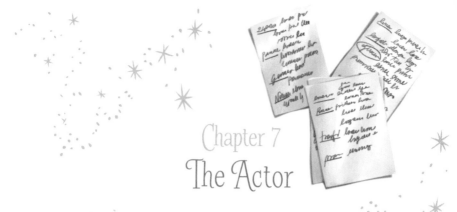

Chapter 7
The Actor

Belle lay awake for most of the night, trying to come up with a plan. She needed to let the village know the bookshop wasn't abandoned. But the town wasn't going to listen to her—she was only a child. The baker hardly listened when she ordered a loaf of bread.

She had to start with people who *might* listen to her, people her own age. The only problem was that right now, no one her age seemed interested in listening to her either. But she was determined to try.

The next day after school, Belle stayed in the schoolyard instead of going to the bookshop. She started with Claudette, Laurette, and Paulette. Belle told them about the amazing stories in the bookshop, but the triplets wouldn't hear another word when they realized it was the "haunted" bookshop.

Next, Belle found Nicolas and Marian. She tried to tell them about the many fascinating books on history, politics, and government at Hugo's, but they wouldn't listen. They were too busy trying to convince everyone to sign their petitions.

Then Belle tried her classmates who were somersaulting down the hill. Juliet's hair was full of twigs and leaves. She listened to what Belle had to say, but she wasn't interested— she found books "boring." Belle didn't bother telling Thomas about the shop. She figured he would only tease her.

Morton sat under his tree. Belle approached him carefully and sat down. "Listen, Morton. I know you prefer being alone, but I have to tell you something. There's an excellent bookshop in the village.

The one that everyone thinks is haunted and abandoned. But it's not. Any story you could dream of reading is there. Do you want to come see it with me?" Belle asked, ready for another rejection.

"Yes," Morton answered.

Belle stared at him in shock. He didn't seem like the type to tease. "You do?" she asked.

"That's what I said," Morton replied.

"*Magnifique!* Let's go," Belle said.

The two made their way through the village to the bookshop. As they walked, Belle explained how the shop was facing trouble. Before they went inside, she said,

"We have to save it, Morton. Once you see it, you'll understand."

She opened the door and Morton looked around. "No ghosts," he said.

"Not one ghost. Just books," Belle said.

"Where are the plays?" Morton asked. He didn't look very impressed.

"I'll show you." Belle led Morton to a shelf near the front of the store. Morton pulled a title from the shelf. Then he pulled another, then another, and another, until he had a stack in his arms up to the top of his head.

Belle helped him carry the stack over to a table. "You must really like plays," she said.

Morton didn't answer. He opened one of the plays and began to read.

Belle tapped her foot, waiting. She had expected Morton to say something about the shop. "So, it's a great place, right?"

"Mm, yes," Morton murmured.

"Any ideas on how to save it?"

"Belle." Morton closed the play. "I feel I should be honest. I cannot spend my time planning with you to save this bookshop. I intend to be a famous actor."

"A famous actor?" Belle asked.

"Yes, of the stage. I must focus on that," Morton said.

"Why?" Belle asked.

"Because I enjoy drama," Morton answered, shrugging his shoulders. He returned to his reading.

Belle buried her face in her hands. It was no use. Morton didn't want to help her. And even if he did, she needed more help than one person could offer her.

And then it hit her. Drama? Belle could find drama.

Chapter 8
Hugo's Bookshop Spectacular

"Over there," Belle said. She shuffled toward a spot of grass in the center of the schoolyard and dropped the bag of props onto the ground.

"Here?" Morton asked. "Everyone can see us here."

"That's the point, Morton!" Belle handed him the wooden sword her father had helped her make the night before. Papa was proud. "You should be excited," she continued. "You're the one who wants to be an actor."

"I intended to make my debut at the Comédie-Française, not at the village school." He turned his nose up in the air.

Belle grabbed a paper dragon from the bag and set it aside. "Remember, if we don't save the bookshop, where will you get the plays you need to study?"

Morton sighed. "All right. I already said I'd do this."

Belle shouted as loud as she could: "Ladies and gentlemen! Boys and girls! Gather round for *Hugo's Bookshop Spectacular.*"

The students nearby stopped what they were doing. Belle continued. "We have adventure! We have fantasy! We have romance!" With each line Belle spoke, Morton withdrew a prop from the bag.  He swung the sword for adventure, he flew Belle's doll through the air for fantasy, and he held up a giant paper heart for romance. The students soon trickled over to watch.

Belle's plan was to perform a scene from a story and stop at the most exciting part. She would then tell her schoolmates that the conclusion was only available in the bookshop. She hoped they would be so interested in the characters, the story, and the *drama* that they would have no choice but to go to the bookshop to see how it ended.

When Belle had explained her plan to Morton, he had insisted on performing something by the great playwright Molière. But Belle knew that wouldn't work. She needed something that would please everyone, so she had combined ideas from a few different stories: a fairy tale, a pirate adventure, a romance, and a comedy.

The play ended with Morton the pirate wailing, "Oh, the pain! Oh, how I bleed! Oh, who can save me now?" Belle's doll tried desperately to save him. But Morton was so caught up in his big dramatic moment, Belle had to pull him off the ground to take a bow.

As they bowed, Belle peeked at the crowd. No one was clapping. No one was even smiling. All she saw were shocked faces, wide eyes, and open mouths.

She stood up straight. "If you'd like to know the fate of the pirate and the doll, you'll have to go to Hugo's Books. Thank you!" Belle couldn't look at the audience for another minute. She quickly cast her eyes to the ground, embarrassed, and stuffed the props back into the bag.

Morton kneeled to help her. He didn't

seem to want to face the crowd either. "My career is ruined, Belle," he whispered in a huff. "My talent has just been wasted!"

The two started to leave the schoolyard when someone spoke. "Well, where is it?"

She heard another voice: "The haunted place?"

And another: "At least give us directions!"

Belle turned around. Juliet, Sylvie, and the rest of the children were following her. Even Thomas was trailing the crowd. "This way!" Belle called.

Belle and Morton led their classmates through the village toward the bookshop.

Chapter 9
A Story for Everyone

Though there had been chatting and horseplay all the way to the bookshop, Belle's classmates fell quiet once they were inside. Belle imagined they were as surprised and enchanted as she had been.

"Where's the story, Belle?" Thomas stepped forward from the group. "You promised us the ending." He craned his neck, searching the shop as though he believed the story would fly off a shelf.

"Oh, right, the story." Belle was in trouble. How would she explain to everyone that there was no ending to the story she'd performed, because it had come from her imagination rather than any one book?

Hugo came out from the back of the shop. "What do we have here?"

"These are my classmates," Belle explained. "They want to know the ending to the story I told them about. The funny adventure with the doll, the dragon, and the pirate."

Hugo raised her eyebrows. She knew there was no such book.

"I need to know if the pirate dies!" Thomas demanded.

Belle mouthed the word *help* at Hugo.

"Why don't you come with me?" Hugo told Thomas. "Perhaps it's with the rest of the pirate books."

"There are *more*?" Thomas said. "C'mon!" He motioned to the others and ran after Hugo to the adventure section. The rest of the group began to follow.

Belle pulled Morton aside. "We have to do something," she whispered.

"Haven't I done enough?" Morton rolled his eyes.

Belle spotted Nicolas and Marian.

They'd stopped on the way to the adventure section, arguing about whether pirates should be considered heroes or villains. Belle grabbed a book from a shelf nearby and shoved it into Morton's hands. "Oh, what do you have there, Morton?" she asked loudly.

"*The Art of Debate,*" he read, thumbing through the pages.

Nicolas peered over Morton's shoulder. "Could I take a look at that?" he asked. Marian bounded over.

"Morton loves this section. He'll tell you all about it," Belle said. Morton glared at her as Marian and Nicolas began to pound him with questions.

Belle ran to catch up with the others. She had to get Sylvie and the triplets away from the adventure section or they'd never stick around.

"Sylvie!" Belle waved her down.

Sylvie, Claudette, Laurette, and Paulette turned around. "I thought we were going to find the story about the magic doll. What's all this about pirates and knights?" Claudette asked Belle.

"The book you want is actually over here," Belle said. She led the girls to the next aisle. As they were walking, Belle used her foot to knock a book off one of the lower shelves. "Oops," she said, picking it up. "It's some book about royal dresses from the last century. That's not what we're looking for." Belle leaned over to put the book back onto the shelf.

"Wait!" Claudette took the book from her hands. Belle was relieved.

"This section is full of boring old books about fashion and costumes and . . ." Belle stopped talking. Laurette and Paulette were already rummaging through the other books on the shelf. Claudette sat down on the floor to look through the pages of the royal dress book. Her sisters gathered around her.

"Enjoy," Belle said. She left the aisle, pleased she'd distracted everyone from her made-up story. Well, almost everyone.

"Belle!" Sylvie ran up behind her. "I'd still like to know how that story ends."

Belle glanced around to make sure no one was listening. "Sylvie, I have to tell you something. But please don't tell the others."

Sylvie crossed her arms. "I'll decide that after I hear what it is."

"There is no story. I mean, not one story. I kind of took a bunch of different story ideas, put them together, and made a new story," Belle confessed.

"Really?" Sylvie asked, furrowing her brow.

"The bookshop is going to close. No one

was listening to me," Belle said. "I had to do something to get you all here, and it worked. Everyone's forgotten about the story and found books they like even better."

"You made that story up?" Sylvie asked. "That's amazing."

"It is?" Belle was surprised.

"It is!" Sylvie said, looking proudly around the bookshop.

Belle couldn't believe what Sylvie was saying. "Thank you."

"I really did want to know what happened in the story, though." Sylvie frowned.

"I'll work on the ending," Belle said. "You'll be the first person I tell it to."

"Deal," Sylvie agreed.

Belle left Sylvie alone to browse. She found Hugo sorting books in the back. "You have a lot of friends," Hugo said.

Friends? Belle thought. A pleasant hush had fallen over the store as everyone read. Maybe her classmates were her friends.

Maybe she had more in common with them than she'd realized.

"I guess I do," Belle said. "They didn't want to come at first, but now that they're here . . . Look." She motioned toward them. "They love it. Doesn't this show you? The shop can be saved."

"I doubt the children have money to spend on books," Hugo said.

"I suppose not." Belle hadn't thought about that. "This is just the beginning. We'll tell everyone in the village, too!"

Hugo placed a hand on Belle's shoulder. "Tell your friends they can each pick out a book to keep."

"Thank you!" Belle was thrilled.

"It's no trouble. They need to be cleared out for Madame Beaumont before she takes over anyway," Hugo replied.

It was clear that the attention from her classmates alone wouldn't save the shop. Belle had a lot more planning and a lot more work to do to prove to Hugo that the bookshop had a future. But as Hugo walked away, Belle thought she caught a glimpse of something unexpected: a smile. And that was something to fight for.

Chapter 10
Worth Fixing

Belle's classmates started joining her at the bookshop after school. Maybe they wanted more free books, but Belle was happy they were there.

As they all walked together each day, Belle told them that Hugo was going to close the shop if business didn't pick up soon. They were eager to help. She didn't tell them the part about Madame Beaumont buying the place, or the fact that Hugo didn't even seem to *want* to keep the shop open. Belle didn't want the cause to seem hopeless.

Each afternoon, Hugo, Belle, and her classmates worked. They dusted the book covers and the shelves until they looked new. They swept and mopped the floors so well, they could see their reflections. They cleaned the dirt from the stained-glass windows, letting the colored sunlight in. Belle's father came to help with the larger repairs, such as fixing the lamps and the cracks in the walls. He took down the boards from the broken window and replaced the glass.

One day Thomas went down to the basement to see if it needed to be cleaned. Moments later Belle saw him run back upstairs, frightened. He closed the basement door. Belle heard hisses coming from below.

"I see you found Tom." Belle giggled.

Thomas noticed Belle watching him, and his face turned red. "What? I'm Tom."

"That's the cat's name, too," Belle said.

"That cat can't have my name! Who does he think he is?" Thomas drew a paper sword from his belt. He'd made it a few days earlier while playing pirates with his friends.

"He's really friendly if you aren't calling him names and tying blindfolds around his head," Belle said.

Thomas eyed the basement door. "That filthy cat can stay in the basement. It's nicer up here anyway."

He was right. The shop looked so good that Belle was starting to forget it had ever been forgotten. It looked the way Belle imagined it had years ago, when Roselle was still around.

"My mother is always saying this building is a waste of space that's just gathering dust," Thomas said. "She's going to be really happy to see what we've done. I know it." He jiggled the doorknob, making sure the basement door stayed closed.

Belle held back another giggle. "You should invite her to come see it."

"She's always busy," Thomas said. "I don't think she'd drop everything to come look at books."

As everyone started to head home, an idea popped into Belle's brain. This was it: the next step of her plan.

"Get everyone together," she told Thomas. "I have an idea."

Belle's classmates joined her outside at the front of the shop. Hugo lingered nearby.

Belle waited until she had everyone's

attention. "I want to plan a grand reopening party for the shop," she announced. Squeals of glee burst from the group. "That is, if it's all right with Hugo?" She crossed her fingers.

All eyes turned to Hugo. "You children can plan your party," she said. "Be my guests."

"When?" Nicolas asked.

"Soon! Very soon," Belle said. Hugo had been giving away books every day. It was a nice treat, but if it continued, there wouldn't be any books left.

"Saturday?" Thomas called out. "I love Saturdays."

Belle glanced at Hugo. She shrugged, which Belle took as a yes. "Yes! Saturday," she said. "That's in a few days, so we have to move quickly. Invite your parents. Invite your friends. Invite anyone you can think of!"

"I'll take to the streets and mobilize the people!" Marian shouted.

"If she's taking to the streets, then I'll take to the rooftops!" Nicolas cried.

"No, don't go on any rooftops. That sounds dangerous. But I like your spirit," Belle said.

Marian and Nicolas grinned.

"I can provide the entertainment," Morton piped up. "I've been practicing my miming."

"Great, Morton!" Belle said.

"I can bring pastries," Juliet suggested. Her father was the baker.

"I'll make decorations," Sylvie said.

"Me too," Claudette, Laurette, and Paulette said in chorus.

"Magnifique!" Belle said. She couldn't believe she had a team as excited and hopeful about saving the bookshop as she was. She wasn't doing this alone. "Let's get started!"

The children broke off into groups, talking about the party. Hugo headed for the back of the shop.

Belle caught up with her before she disappeared into the basement. "Hugo, don't you want to help with the planning?"

Hugo paused at the door. "There were plenty of parties in the past, you know. This used to be the place everyone wanted to be."

"It can still be that place," Belle said.

"It can't be the way it was. No one wants to be here," Hugo said.

"*You* don't seem like you want to be here. You spend most of your time down in the basement." Belle's voice trembled. She knew her words might upset Hugo.

Hugo blinked in surprise. "It's for the best. History, politics—there are newspapers for that. The stories in here, they just meddle with young minds like yours."

Belle hated it when Hugo spoke that way. "I know you don't really believe that. I know part of you still cares, or you wouldn't keep buying new books."

"Old habits, I guess." Hugo turned the doorknob.

Belle still wasn't getting through. What was the point of all this planning, all this work, if Hugo's heart wasn't even in it? Something was broken in Hugo, and Belle had to fix it.

She put her hand on the door, blocking Hugo's way. "I know you're sad that your daughter left. I get sad when I miss my mother, and I didn't even know her. But your daughter left because she had big dreams, and I have big dreams, too. I used to think that made me different and strange. But when I came here and found all these books, I realized there are places in the world where I belong, even if I haven't found them yet. Your daughter's dreams brought her a happy ending. And maybe your happy ending is still here in this shop."

Belle held her breath. Hugo just stared at Belle's hand blocking the door. Belle let her arm drop to her side.

"Grand reopening or grand closing. It doesn't matter." Hugo disappeared down the stairs.

Chapter 11
The Grand Reopening

When Saturday arrived, Belle got to the bookshop at dawn. The grand reopening was scheduled to begin at noon, but she wanted to make sure everything was perfect. All of the books were arranged on straight shelves, thanks to her father. The wood, marble, and glass were so clean they sparkled. Belle knew she was standing in a bookshop in her small provincial town, but it felt so much grander than that. To her, the shop looked like a place where magic could happen. As Belle watched Hugo stroll through the aisles, observing the changes, she hoped some of that feeling was still alive in the woman's heart as well.

By eleven-thirty Belle's classmates had all arrived. Morton set up a small stage near the entrance. Sylvie and the triplets hung colorful paper flowers around the shop. Nicolas helped Juliet arrange dozens of delicious-looking pastries on a table, which Marian promptly rearranged. Even Hugo helped, bringing up jugs of water and chairs from the basement. "Left over from the old days," she said. Thomas made sure the basement door was securely closed after each and every trip.

Just before noon, Belle's father entered the shop, his face hidden behind a giant arrangement of flowers.

"Oh, Papa!" Belle gasped at the beautiful bouquet. Her father was holding at least a dozen perfect red roses.

Maurice peered at her between the thorny stems. "Your mother always loved roses. Picking them and admiring them, but most of all, giving them." He kissed his daughter on the cheek. "I'm afraid I didn't bring a vase."

"I can help with that." Hugo appeared at his side. She scooped the roses into a glass vase and set it down on the cashier's desk. "What do you think?" she asked Belle.

"Lovely," Belle said.

Hugo leaned down and sniffed the roses. "That brings back some memories," she said.

"Good ones, I hope," Belle said.

Hugo gazed at Belle. Her face looked sad.

Oh no, Belle thought. But then the corners of Hugo's mouth curled. She smiled. A real, true smile.

"Yes. Good memories," Hugo said. "Now, let's keep these doors open so everyone knows where the party is."

Belle ran to the entrance. She swung the doors wide and propped them open with two large encyclopedias. In a few minutes it would be noon.

Within an hour Belle had lost count of how many people were there. The place was full, and the grand reopening couldn't have been going any better.

Belle darted around the shop, making sure everything was going smoothly. Grown-ups looked over the books and admired the beauty of the building. Younger children listened to Morton read stories aloud—he'd given up on the mime act when he realized no one was paying attention. Her classmates gave their parents tours of the shop and pointed out their favorite books to strangers. Belle's father stayed busy behind the cashier's desk, selling books to a growing line of customers.

Hugo didn't disappear into the basement once. Instead she mingled with the guests, and her smile even appeared a few more times. Belle paused to watch her talk to a young girl Belle's age about a book of fairy tales. It was the same book that Belle, and then Sylvie, had read on their first days in the shop. Hugo had to be having a change of heart. Belle was sure her plan had been a success.

But then an angry Madame Beaumont marched through the doors. She headed directly toward Hugo and wagged her finger. Hugo left the girl with the book and followed Madame Beaumont. The two women went into the basement.

Rats, Belle thought. How could she hear what they were saying if they were in the basement? She raced outside and around the building to the basement window. She crouched beside it, straining to listen.

"The children wanted to have a party." That was Hugo's voice.

"I see what you're doing, Hugo. You're making one last attempt to save your business." Madame Beaumont. Her voice had such a nasty tone.

"I wasn't trying to do anything. But it seems I may have been wrong about the village's need for a bookshop. About my need . . ." Hugo's voice drifted off. Then she spoke again. "Everyone's so happy to be here. I thought they'd forgotten."

"They had forgotten, and they will
again. I hope for your sake that you sell all
the books today. I still want them gone,"
Madame Beaumont said.

Belle pulled away from the window. She
couldn't listen anymore. She couldn't believe
it. So many people loved this shop now. How

was it possible that their love wasn't enough to save it? Belle had fixed what was broken, but it was too late.

Chapter 12

A Dreamer and a Doer

Belle went back inside the shop. She figured she should enjoy it for the little time she had left. She wandered over to the adventure section, where Thomas was playing pirates with some other boys.

"Belle!" Thomas shouted when he saw her. "Have you seen my mother?"

"I've never met your mother. What does she look like?" Belle asked.

Thomas scrunched his face in thought. "She's always got some fancy outfit on. Her hair is all loopy." Thomas swirled his hands around his head.

"You mean curly?" Belle asked.

"Yeah, that. I was sure I saw her go off with that old bookshop lady. Maybe not," Thomas said.

Belle's mind began to race, putting two and two together. "Thomas, is your mother Madame Beaumont?"

"Sure is," Thomas said.

"But your last name is Gagne," Belle said.

"Yeah," Thomas said. "That's our family's

last name. My mother likes to use *her* father's last name, though. She says Beaumont is more extinguished."

"I think you mean distinguished," Belle corrected.

"Sorry, I don't read your fancy dictionaries, Belle," Thomas said.

Belle realized that there was still a chance. She'd gotten through to Hugo and the village. Maybe there was a way to get through to Madame Beaumont, too. Of course, it was just Belle's luck that she'd have to rely on Thomas.

"Thomas, you have to go get your mother and give her a tour of the bookshop.

Show her how much you like it here," Belle said. "She's in the basement."

"The basement?" Thomas's face went white.

"Are you really afraid of a cat?" Belle was losing her patience.

"That's not a cat; it's a beast!"

"A beast that shares your name. How scary can someone named Tom really be?"

"Hey, I can be scary." Thomas tried to growl, but it sounded more like a meow.

"Very scary. Tom the cat doesn't stand a chance," Belle said. "Now go!"

Thomas touched the paper sword he kept tied to his belt before heading off. He

opened the basement door and returned
a few moments later, dragging Madame
Beaumont by the arm.

"Tom-Tom, I was in the middle of an
important meeting," Madame Beaumont
complained.

"I want to show you around, Mother.
I read these books—look!" Thomas ran

around, pulling Madame Beaumont to the adventure section. He handed her a book.

"You read this?" she asked him.

"You bet I did, and two more! Isn't it great?" Thomas practically jumped up and down as he watched his mother flip through the book.

"It is, dear." Madame Beaumont seemed surprised. "It's a shame that—"

"Régine!" Three women scurried up to Madame Beaumont, books in one hand, skirts in the other.

"Ladies," Madame Beaumont greeted them.

"Have you seen this place?" one of them asked.

"Who knew we had such a center of history and knowledge in our little village? I thought it shut down years ago, but it's just like it was when I was a child," the second said.

"The culture here," the third woman said, fanning herself. "It's so inspiring!"

"Yes, it's a lovely building," Madame Beaumont said.

"Not just the building, Régine. Think of the possibilities," the first woman said. "Those literary salons we've been hearing stories about? They're all the rage in Paris.

This would be the perfect place to hold our own."

Belle watched Madame Beaumont. She noticed Hugo had joined them; she was standing back and listening to the women speak.

"There'd be plenty of room for a gathering if we got rid of the books—" Madame Beaumont began.

"No!" the women cried.

"No!" Thomas shouted.

"We need the books so we have topics to discuss," the second woman said.

"Mama, what's a salon?" Thomas asked.

The first woman answered. "It's a lovely,

elegant affair where ladies like your mother, and us, gather to discuss art and global affairs and—"

"Never mind," Thomas said, scowling. "I'll stick to pirates." He ran off to find his friends.

"It sounds very exciting," Belle said. "Very Parisian," she added.

Madame Beaumont cleared her throat and looked at Hugo. "This shop has suddenly become so popular, both with my son and my friends." She paused. "I'm glad you're back in business, Hugo. It would be a shame to keep hiding it away from our village and our children."

Belle's hands flew to her mouth, trying to quiet her squeal of joy. Hugo bowed her head, an enormous smile on her face.

"It would be a shame indeed. I look forward to your salons, ladies." Hugo nodded at the three women as they walked away, heading for the pastry table. Madame Beaumont followed. As she passed, Hugo whispered, just loud enough for Belle to hear, "Does this mean you'll tear up the paperwork for the sale?"

Madame Beaumont patted her curls, making sure they were all in place. "I don't have much of a choice, do I? Just do me a favor, if you could. Don't tell anyone I planned to get rid of the books. I have a feeling that would make me very . . . unpopular."

Hugo winked. "It's our secret," she said. Madame Beaumont shuffled off in the direction of her friends.

"You did it," Hugo said to Belle.

"*We* did it," Belle said.

Hugo shook her head. "I'd given up. I didn't think I'd find my love for this store again, but now . . . you've shown me that it never left. It was just hiding under the dust."

Belle grinned. "I'm sorry your daughter isn't here to see how great it looks."

"She'll be back to see it someday," Hugo said. "According to her letters."

"You read the letters?" Belle asked.

"Last night. You gave quite the speech," Hugo said. "And you were right. She's happy. It's time for me to be happy, too."

Belle couldn't resist. She flung her arms out and wrapped Hugo in a hug.

Hugo patted Belle on the back. "It's not the end yet. There's plenty of work ahead."

"I can help," Belle said. "I don't mind working. Not if it's something I love."

"I don't either. But today it's time to celebrate." Hugo held her hand out to Belle, and Belle took it.

They joined the others near the front of the shop. Belle left Hugo to mingle and went to find her father.

"There won't be a sale. The bookshop is going to stay open!" she told him.

Maurice smiled down at her. "My Belle. I'm so proud of you. Look at what you created here."

Belle blushed. "I didn't create it, Papa. It's Hugo's shop."

"But you found the missing pieces," her father said. "And that's the mark of a dreamer and a doer. Otherwise known as an inventor."

Belle looked at the pieces she'd assembled.

Morton was trying out his mime act one more time. Sylvie and the triplets were reading books to their dolls. Nicolas and Marian were debating village politics in front of Madame Beaumont, much to her displeasure. Thomas was petting Tom the cat, who'd come up from the basement. And Hugo . . . Hugo was smiling and watching it all.

Belle swelled with pride. In the bookshop, she had found a place where she could be herself. And now she had many people with whom she could share her special place.

The pieces fit perfectly.